Wanted
Dead or Alive

Written by Cecilia Sanders
Illustrated by Maria Westy Bush

AuthorHouse™
1663 Liberty Drive
Bloomington, IN 47403
www.authorhouse.com
Phone: 1-800-839-8640

First published by AuthorHouse   9/8/2010

ISBN: 978-1-4520-7023-0 (sc)

Printed in the United States of America

This book is printed on acid-free paper.

authorHOUSE®

Markwongnark

Wanted
Dead or Alive

Written by Cecilia Sanders
Illustrated by Maria Westy Bush

WANTED
DEAD OR ALIVE

Foster Fox was very proud of his fruit and vegetable garden. He had rows and rows of tall, sweet, yellow corn. Next to the corn plants was a bushy row of juicy red tomatoes. Green bean plants crawled up the fence that surrounded the garden. Each plant wore hundreds of crisp, thin beans.

Squash plants, eggplants, cabbage, beets and many other vegetables and fruit trees thrived in Foster's well groomed garden. Foster Fox's most prized fruit trees were the persimmon trees that bordered his spacious yard.

Foster arose very early each morning to weed and irrigate his garden. When his chores were done, he would pick the fruits and vegetables and take them to the market to sell.

Foster's favorite thing to do in the early morning was to simply walk through his garden and admire the beautiful plants. He felt greatly rewarded for all the hard work and the time that he spent tending the garden.

On his way back to the house, Foster reached up and picked a plump persimmon from the lower branches of his favorite fruit tree. He savored the sweet taste of the perfectly ripe fruit while leaning against the trunk of the tree.

"Oh, soooooo delicious," he thought as he nearly dozed off in the warm rays of the early sun.

About a mile down the lane from where Foster Fox lived, another family kept residence in a tree that was over a hundred years old. The tall tree had graceful, thick branches covered with leaves to shade them. The best thing about the tree was that it had a large dead branch that was hollow inside. It was a perfect place for an opossum family to live. Foster was unaware of his neighbors.

Mrs. Opossum had three children. There were two boys. Their names were Peter and Paul. There was also a sweet little girl named Patsy.

When Peter, Paul and Patsy were very young, Mrs. Opossum taught them things that they would need to know when they grew up and left home to make lives of their own. One of the most important skills that an opossum needs to know is how to play dead. Mrs. Opossum taught them this skill by playing games.

"I am a hungry mountain lion," she would say as she leaped at them when they were not looking. All at the same time Peter, Paul and Patsy would fall over on their sides and lie very still with their mouths gaping open showing the fifty sharp teeth inside.

Mrs. Opossum taught them how to breathe from deep inside. By doing this, the three little opossums looked just as if they were dead.

"Good job!" Exclaimed Mrs. Opossum, "If I didn't know better I would feel sorry for you." Mrs. Opossum leaned over and whispered in Patsy's ear, "Try to breathe a little deeper Patsy." "Okay Mom," she replied. Mrs. Opossum didn't want Patsy's brothers teasing her.

One evening Peter, Paul and Patsy were allowed to walk to a friends' house. As they left their tree house, Mrs. Opossum waved at them and told them to be careful.

"If something frightens you remember what I taught you to do," she told them.

"Okay Mom, don't worry," chimed the trio of opossums. They were on their way to visit Skeeter. Skeeter was a skunk. He was shiny black with a snow white cap on his head that stretched all the way down his back and spread into his bushy tail.

Skeeter's Mom also taught him what to do when he got frightened. All that he had to do was to raise his bushy tail and a terrible, horrible, awful smell was everywhere. The odor was sooooo bad that nothing could get close enough to harm little Skeeter.

After getting bored at Skeeter's house the little skunk and Peter, Paul and Patsy went for a walk to see what was at the far end of the lane. It was late evening when Peter, Paul, Patsy and Skeeter passed by a farm house.

"Yap, yap, yap, yap," said the small furry animal as it bounded toward them. "Yap, yap, yap." The three opossums pretended to die. Plop, plop, plop, went the three little grey bodies with long rat tails. They were scared to death by the barking dog. Their sharp teeth glistened from their gaping mouths as they lay motionless on the ground.

Skeeter also did as he was taught. Soon the terrible, horrible, awful smell permeated the air.

"Yap, yap, yap," said the small furry animal as it raced away from the scene. When the dog was out of sight, Peter, Paul and Patsy pinched their noses shut as they giggled and stood up.

"WOW! It does work," said Peter

Boy, I'll say it does," said Paul.

"Giggle, giggle, giggle," said Patsy.

"Skeeter, who taught you how to do that," they asked him while still holding their noses.

"My Mom," Skeeter said proudly.

Quite satisfied with their skills, the four friends continued their walk down the lane. By dark, Peter, Paul, Patsy and Skeeter had come to the edge of Foster Fox's property. The beautiful persimmon trees instantly attracted the little opossums.

"Look," said Peter. "Mom buys these at the market."

"Yum," said Paul. "There must be a million of them."

Patsy was already nibbling on one of the tasty fruits that had fallen from the tree. Persimmons were one of their favorite treats.

Skeeter too, thought they were really good.
The foursome headed for home before becoming sick from eating too many persimmons.

Early the next morning Foster Fox was out doing his chores and enjoying his garden. As he passed by the persimmon trees, he noticed that there were several partially eaten fruits on the ground. He stooped down to get a better look.

"Hmmm," he said to himself. "I wonder who has been eating my persimmons."

Nothing happened for the next few nights. Every morning Foster checked the trees. Nothing was amiss.

The next night Peter, Paul, Patsy and Skeeter came back to Foster's yard to eat persimmons. When their tummies were full, they rested before starting for home. On this night, however, Foster was looking for a hoe that he had left in the yard. He heard a sound near the persimmon trees and went to see what it was.

When the opossums heard him coming they all played dead.

Plop, plop, plop, went the falling bodies. Skeeter raised his bushy tail, let out the terrible, horrible, awful smell and scampered into the tall grass and out of sight.

When Foster saw the three little dead opossums he felt very bad. Holding his nose because of the terrible, horrible, awful smell, he knelt down to look at them.

"Oh my," he said aloud. "The poor little things, they must have eaten too many persimmons and died."

One by one he carried the stiff little bodies and laid them peacefully under a tree. He would come back at daylight and bury them.

As soon as Foster Fox was out of sight, the three little opossums sat up. They were laughing so hard that their tummies hurt. Skeeter joined them and the four giggling friends started for home.

"Boy did we trick him," said Peter.

"We sure did," replied Paul.

Patsy was giggling so hard that she couldn't say anything.

The next morning Foster Fox got up extra early to take care of the poor dead little opossums. The usually happy fox was not looking forward to what he had to do.

When Foster got to the tree where he had laid the dead opossums the night before, he discovered that they were gone.

"It was dark," he thought. "Maybe it wasn't this tree." He looked under each persimmon tree. He couldn't find the opossums anywhere.

Foster thought and thought all day long about what had happened the night before. He decided to stay up late that night to see if he could solve the mystery.

For two nights Foster watched the persimmon trees. He hid behind the bushy tomato plants so he could not be seen. Finally on the third night Foster heard voices coming down the lane. He crouched down even lower and peeked over the plants.

Peter, Paul, Patsy and Skeeter came into his view. The three little opossums scurried up the persimmon tree. Peter picked a persimmon and tossed it down to Skeeter. Skeeter couldn't climb trees. When the three persimmon stuffed opossums came down the trunk of the tree to the ground Foster made a noise.

Plop, plop, plop, went the opossums. Skeeter scampered into the tall grass leaving behind the terrible, horrible, awful smell.

"So that's what is going on," thought Foster. Once again Foster Fox picked up the three "dead" opossums. He laid them under the tree and went back to hide behind the tomato plants. When the opossums thought he was gone, they all sat up and laughed and laughed and laughed.

Foster Fox was not very pleased about the opossums and the skunk trying to out-fox him. He spent the next day making a sign and ignoring his usual garden chores. When Foster finished the sign he left for town.

The next day Mrs. Opossum, Peter, Paul and Patsy went to town to go to the market.

"If you are good I will buy you each a persimmon," she told them.

The three looked at each other and smiled.

"We would like that," they said. Patsy started to giggle.

"Shhhhhh," said Peter and Paul.

After shopping at the fruit and vegetable market Mrs. Opossum and her family stopped at the post office to mail a letter.

WANTED
DEAD OR ALIVE

FOR STEALING PERSIMMONS

REWARD

Foster Fox

Right inside the Post Office was a large sign. Mrs.Opossum nearly died when she saw it.

"Can you explain this?" asked Mrs. Opossum as she looked down at the three startled youngsters whose faces were staring down at them from the wall.

"We think so," they all said at the same time.

Peter, Paul and Patsy told their mother about finding the persimmon trees with their friend Skeeter.

"We didn't think anyone saw us," said Paul.
"And you think you can out-fox a fox?" said Mrs. Opossum. "Don't be silly."

"Come with me," she said.

The three little opossums obediently followed their mother. Down the lane they went to pick up Skeeter.

"You have been caught, Skeeter. Tell your mother that you are coming with me," said Mrs.Opossum to the little skunk.

"Yes Ma'am," replied Skeeter.

"Where are we going?" asked Patsy.

"To apologize to Mr. Fox," answered her mother. Silently the four little tricksters followed Mrs. Opossum down the long lane to Foster Fox's house.

There was nothing in the world that could make Patsy giggle right now. They were very embarrassed.

When they came to Foster's house, Mrs. Opossum marched them in front of her, stood on the porch and rang the doorbell.

Foster couldn't believe his eyes when he answered the door. Before he could speak, Mrs. Opossum said, "We have something to tell you Mr. Fox."

"We are very sorry that we stole your persimmons Mr. Fox," stuttered Peter.

"We know better than to do what we did, Mr. Fox, I am so sorry," said Paul.

"I am sorry, Mr. Fox, very sorry," said Patsy with tears forming in her eyes.

"Mr. Fox," said Skeeter. "I am sorry about the terrible, horrible, awful smell and for stealing the persimmons."

"Please forgive us," they all said.

"Well," said Mr. Fox. "I appreciate that you turned yourselves in. However, I think you should be punished for what you did."

Mrs. Opossum had an idea. "Maybe they could help you do your garden chores."

"That is a great idea." He replied.

So for the next week, Peter, Paul, Patsy and Skeeter got out of bed before the sun was awake. They walked down the long lane to Foster Fox's house.

There they worked all day long pulling weeds, watering plants and picking fruits and vegetables to take to the market.

They were so tired at the end of the day that they fell into bed and slept soundly until morning.

After a week of hard, tiring work, Peter, Paul, Patsy and Skeeter learned a very valuable lesson. They realized that to have nice things and to be proud of the things that you have takes a lot of hard work and dedication. Stealing the persimmons was easy. It wasn't hard work. They felt very bad about what they had done and they would never do such a terrible thing again.

The day after the four youngsters finished their work for Foster Fox, a very special package was delivered to their tree. It was addressed to Peter, Paul and Patsy Opossum and Skeeter Skunk. Inside the box was a basketful of perfect persimmons. The card read, "Thank You," Foster Fox.

The four little friends leaned against the trunk
of the tree, enjoying their reward for being
honest. Patsy just couldn't keep from giggling.

Opossums have the special talent to play dead when they are threatened. Skunks emit a terrible odor when they are threatened. Each is a talent for self defense.

Use your special talents to do good, not to cheat.

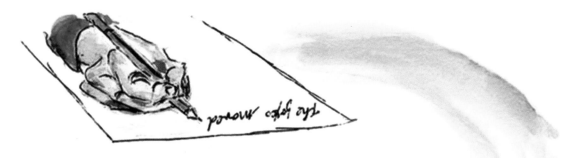

About the Author

Cecilia Sanders has helped wildlife as a wildlife reha-
bilitator for more than twenty years and has worked
with thousands of wild orphans. A series of children's
stories were created by witnessing the fascinating hab-
its of the animals who have shared her life.

About the Illustrator

Maria Westy Bush lives on a Colorado ranch. She has
a Master of Fine Arts degree from the University Of
Washington and has taught art students from age
three to ninety, in private and in public schools.
She has also taught Art Appreciation for the Adams
State Prison College Program.
A cancer survivor, she has had her artwork exhibited
from coast to coast and border to border. Her two
sons, now successful in their forties, have been the de-
manding and beneficial critics of her illustrations.

CPSIA information can be obtained
at www.ICGtesting.com
Printed in the USA
LVIW022052180213

320644LV00004B